The Initiate Rises
The Twisted Society

Cristina Lollabrigida

This is for the readers who want a story that will tear their soul from their body and torture them with a morally grey hero who turns pitch black for the woman he loves.

Trigger/content Warning

Trigger/content Warning

Triggers may include:

Strong language, graphic sexual content (including bondage, primal, cum play, blood play, among others), non-consensual sexual content, torture, offensive religious imagery, blood/gore, unalives for her, cannibalism, attempted infanticide, and more.

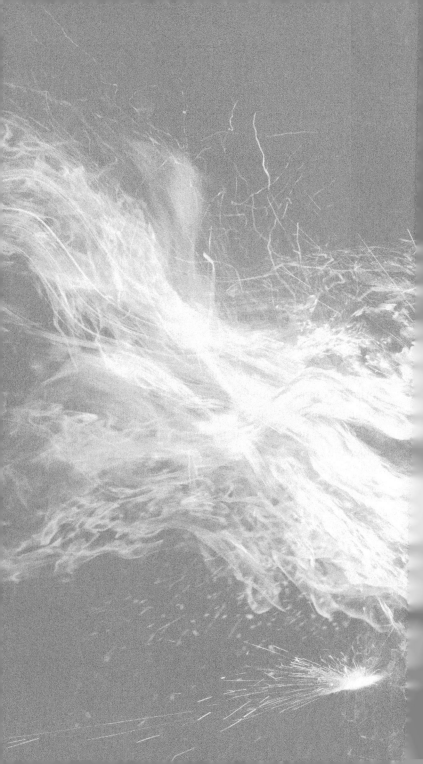

Lucifer

LOVE IS A FALLACY, as Lucien discovered while cradling the body of his dying lover after their child was ripped from her womb. He promised forever to an angel and damned her to Hell. He had failed in his duties as both the son of Satan and a human. Their blood bond meant their hearts would forever beat in tandem. His heart slowed as Sadie's life force slipped away. If hers stopped, so would his, and he would face a fate worse than death. There was no time to lose.

His body rippled as he lost control of his emotions. His demonic self had already stolen the life of an innocent. Beatrice's body remained crumpled on the cold, hard ground where it had fallen, and her soul was already in Hell.

In his anguish, Lucifer took on his angelic form. He tore his shirt a moment before wings sprouted from his back. One was large and black with coarse feathers. The other was snow white with long, delicate feathers.

He reached up and plucked a white feather from his wing. The pain was excruciating, but it paled in comparison to the pain in his heart. The feather was soon drenched in Sadie's crimson blood.

If anyone were to stumble upon them, they would lose their mind as they gazed upon him. This form wasn't meant for human eyes—except for Sadie. They were bound: heart, body, and soul.

"Mother!" Lucifer screamed into the wind as he plunged the quill into his heart.

The falling snow froze before his eyes, hanging in suspended animation.

"Mother!" he bellowed. "I need your help."

The snow swirled around him in a frenzy, trapping him in its vortex. A portal opened before his eyes. The song of heavenly hosts wasn't meant for his unworthy ears, so he was forcibly deafened. As the son of Satan, he was condemned by holy beings, and he fucking despised them for it.

His heart had grown embittered toward that side of himself as a child. His big brother bullied him for thousands of years. Cain was born as his father took the form of a serpent and tempted a woman in a garden. He fucked her beneath an apple tree and left her with the choice to eat the ripened fruit and bear his heir or die from his venom. Naturally, she chose the former. Cain was born with a twin, similar to Sadie. Like Constance, the elder twin was shrouded in darkness that slowly poisoned their souls, twisting them in insanity until they lashed out in malice to destroy their sibling.

Unfortunately for Abel, no one was around to protect him. He was brutally stabbed with a broken bone shard. Lucifer had thought choosing Sadie as the Winter Maiden would save her from a similar fate. They have a saying about good intentions for a reason.

A moment later, a delicate touch caressed his shoulder. He turned his face into his mother's ethereal gown, clinging to her like a small child. His tears soaked the thin fabric, making it translucent.

She stroked his hair lightly. Her voice was barely a whisper as she spoke. "You're sobbing, Lucifer. You haven't cried since you were a child."

The last time he cried was when his mother ascended and left him alone. As the son of the Devil and a birthright Angel, there was light and darkness in him. He had buried the goodness and embraced his demonic nature until Sadie awakened feelings and desires that were foreign to him.

She loved him despite his origins. He'd warned her what would happen if she gave him her heart. Now he would do anything to save her.

"Save her, Mother," he begged. "Please."

His mother gazed at Sadie for the first time. Her chest heaved as she made little gurgling sounds as though each breath was more painful than the last. The angel caressed Sadie's forehead with a gentle hand.

"I can't, Lucifer. It's her time."

Lucifer's roar echoed around them. Snow tumbled down the hill, but they were protected in the vortex.

"I need a fucking miracle. You owe me. The angels owe me

for taking you away. I need Sadie! You must save her. I know you can do it. Save her!"

"No," she said softly.

Utter hopelessness threatened to send the devil into a blind rage. Darkness flooded his irises, turning his eyes dark as midnight and his velvety voice became hollow. "I will tear apart the castle, stone by stone. I will find Mrs. Winters and slice her belly open, pull out her entrails, and shit inside them. Then I will burn the wench alive. When I find Constance, I'm going to impale her on a spike, peel her skin off in strips, and feed it to my hounds. I will force her to drink my blood to remain alive for days before throwing her to the wolves and allowing them to ravage her before dragging her into Hell and torturing her myself for eternity. I will murder every man, woman, and child in the village and burn it to ash. These lands will be cursed forevermore."

"Luci–"

"I'm not finished yet," he snarled. "I won't stop until this world is destroyed. I will find my son, because that's the last promise I made to his mother."

The angel's eyes glowed with a blinding white light. "Your child is no longer alive."

Lucifer jumped up. "That's a lie. I can feel his heartbeat like I feel Sadie's."

"Your child–"

He roared again. "Stop saying *my child* in pity. It's my son, and I will find him."

"Your child is in purgatory, Lucifer. I'm sorry, but you know you can't go there."

"No!" he howled in grief.

"While you were throwing your tantrum, the Winter Maiden has taken her last breath."

He stood motionless and placed his hand over his heart, which was no longer beating.

"Bring her back!" he screamed. "Bring her back, goddamn you!"

"I'm sorry," she whispered sympathetically.

Lucifer detonated. He didn't just pluck a white feather out of his wing this time but bellowed as he tore the entire thing out of his back. Blood ran in warm rivulets down his spine, but he was impervious to the agonizing physical pain because the loss of Sadie made him wish he was in oblivion. There was no life without her.

Once the blood stopped, he took a deep breath and tore the black wing out.

"I denounce your kind, Mother," he roared. "I denounce Satan!"

He stood and raised his hands. "I vow to burn this world to ash. It shall know war, destruction, and death. I will destroy The Society, if it's the last thing I do."

Lucifer pulled his dagger from his belt and slit his palm, letting the blood fall onto Sadie's forehead. "I will do it for her."

The angel stroked her son's back. "The pain is fleeting."

He screamed in agony as new wings sprouted from his back. They weren't black or white, but gray—the color of clouds before a storm—and he was the harbinger.

Lilith wasn't impassive as she watched her son's grief; she was forbidden to interfere. A single tear ran down the angel's face, and she raised her palm to catch it.

A golden light engulfed Lilith, illuminating her very skin as though she had swallowed the sun. Her lips moved as she prayed words that Lucifer couldn't hear. It lasted only moments, but it was enough. She held her hand out to her son.

"Place this in her heart. It will reverse the poison that has infected her. No matter what you do, she will die. If you don't want her to ascend and take her place among us, you must drag her to Hell.

"She will be forced into the circles. There will be only one point at which you may interact with her before she ascends or descends into the next ring. Each time you meet, she will experience unbearable pain and suffer death again."

"And how do I save her?"

"Offer her a choice. If she agrees to allow you to take away her memory of the trauma, she will face the next circle. This will continue until her psyche is ready to become whole once more. When she refuses your offer, she will be freed."

"And how long will that take?"

The angel frowned. "You know I can't see that. It's what they call free will. The cycle may last all eternity."

Lucien gazed at Sadie. "How will I know when and where to find her?"

She shook her head and spoke as though the answer was obvious. "Your heart will start beating again."

Thump... thump... He gasped and clutched his chest as his heart started beating again.

"What is this?"

"I am giving you a chance to say goodbye."

Sadie

BEING CHOSEN WASN'T A PRIVILEGE—IT was a death sentence, as Sadie Winters had learned the hard way.

It was her duty to warn the village of those who lived in the castle built into the mountainside. She had discovered their dark secrets while she was their unwitting guest. Now she understood why the sky was always bleak and no Winter Maiden ever returned.

These poor women thought they were receiving a grand offer, but in truth, their families were compensated for their daughters facing slaughter like cattle. Lucien told her he had never participated in the Offering before. She clung to that hope that her baby wouldn't face the same fate.

With her swollen belly, Sadie scaled down the mountain to seek refuge away from the castle. Wolves silently stalked her, but the hunter frightened her most. Cain rode her down on his black stallion, the same she tried to protect moons ago in the village. Was the animal broken of his spirit, or did he fight like hell to survive, like her?

Sadie didn't want to drink the concoction thrust in her face. With a weapon threatening her unborn child, she did the only thing she could to try and keep it safe, and that was to comply.

The Winter Maiden screamed in terror as the knife sliced through her body, cutting her from breast to pubis. The snowy ground was quickly stained red and became slushy from the blood draining from her body.

Excruciating pain turned her vision white, but she clung to consciousness. Constance laughed as she tore the baby from Sadie's womb. A tiny infant, born too soon, wailed as they whisked it away.

Falling in love was the most incredible experience of Sadie's 18 years. Every fiber of her being awoke in her lover's arms. His promises meant nothing now as her heart slowed.

The pillow was wet with tears as Sadie awoke, gasping for breath. She shakily dropped her hands to her belly, no longer swollen with child.

Panic overwhelmed her, causing her to break into a sweat. It wasn't a nightmare—it was real. Sadie had to find Constance and get her baby back.

The vivid memory of hearing her baby's first cries made Sadie's lower lip tremble. How scared and tiny it was without its mother to protect it.

But Sadie wasn't helpless in the snow now. She was in a comfortable bed with silk sheets atop the down mattress. There was no cradle for a baby.

"Lucien!" she sobbed, shaking him awake. "Where's the baby?"

Lucien rolled over with a devil-may-care smile and lazily brushed his hand over her soft stomach.

"What baby?" he asked. "There is no baby, Sadie."

She pushed herself up, wanting to smack him as he wrapped his arm around her bare waist and pulled her against his side.

"Let me go!" she cried, attempting to wiggle out of his grasp. "I have to find my baby."

"Shhh. Calm down, Sadie. You were never with child."

"Why are you lying to me?" she asked through tears.

Something wasn't right. She felt it in her bones. She'd never had a dream as vivid as the nightmare of lying in the freezing snow while her life slowly drifted away. There was no forgetting the wailing newborn Constance clutched to her chest as she turned and ran away.

The devastation on Lucien's face when he had found her shattered her heart into tiny fragmented pieces. She hadn't meant for any of this to happen. She wished she could take away his pain. Even though he smiled at her, she could still see the misery in his eyes.

"Sadie, please." He cupped her cheeks and peppered kisses on her forehead, nose, and lips. "Stay here with me. Let's enjoy the morning together."

"Lucien..."

He'd returned home to see his father and just returned the night before. Though she'd missed his arms and wanted nothing more than to spend the day in bed with him, there was no explaining why her heart felt torn in two.

"Let me make you forget everything, Sadie," Lucien said as he kissed her shoulder and cupped her breast.

She closed her eyes and inhaled his fiery brimstone scent before pushing him away.

"Please, Lucifer."

"Look into my eyes, Sadie," he began. "We have a small amount of time before I have to leave again. I promise you have nothing to worry about. Trust me. It was only a bad dream."

She did trust him with every fiber of her being. Was it possible she was only dreaming, as he said? Did it matter, if they were here together? She couldn't deny that sense of something missing.

"I must not be doing a good job if you still have that frown on your face," he cajoled.

"No, Lucien."

He looked near tears as he said, "Please, Sadie. I need this."

She wanted to weep at the forlorn expression on his face.

"We'll talk after." It wasn't a request.

No matter how often they were together, Sadie was forever in awe that this devil would bow before her. He had the power to take what he wanted, and sometimes, he did. But in moments when he showed her vulnerability, there was no denying the love they shared.

Lucien's hand moved between Sadie's thighs, and soon all coherent thought was pushed from her mind.

"Mmm," she moaned.

"Does that feel good, tulip?"

She nodded and tilted her head for more hungry kisses. Sadie melted into Lucien's chest, becoming pliant to his desire.

"Oh, Lucien. Please..."

"Please what?" he whispered into her ear.

She closed her eyes and released her anxiety, losing herself in sensation.

"I need more."

"Then my distraction is working. Let me give you what you're craving."

There was no doubting what her aching core needed. She craved Lucien's hot manhood, which was throbbing against her lower back. But he was in no rush to give it to her. He dipped two fingers into her dripping slit.

"It's been too long, Sadie."

"We were together all night." Her giggle quickly became a moan when his thumb brushed her clit.

"Are you feeling sassy today, tulip? Do I need to teach your mouth how to behave?"

Lucien's seductive words sent a shiver down her spine. Her chest heaved in excitement as he pinched her nipple and curled his fingers inside her. He shifted his hips, grinding his arousal against her backside. The warmth of Lucien's breath caused goosebumps along her collarbone.

"You're a dream, Sadie Winters."

He lifted her by the hips and guided her onto his cock. She moaned as every inch of him made her deliciously full. When she was fully seated, he grabbed her by the hair and pulled her flush against him.

"You're so fucking tight," he growled into her ear. " I'll never get enough of how eager your cunt is for me."

"Only for you, Lucien," she whined.

"That's right, tulip. Don't forget that."

Her hips rocked back and forth, searching for the perfect rhythm to chase her pleasure. Lucien thrust his hips repeatedly.

Sadie was desperate to gaze at Lucien's face. She wanted to see him, hold him, and kiss him. As usual, he seemed to know her very thoughts. His lips caught hers as she twisted her neck toward him.

She sobbed as she came apart.

"Someday we'll be together forever, Sadie," he promised.

Sadie held that promise close to her heart.

Lucifer

LUCIEN SIGHED WEARILY as his heart slowed. It was time to say goodbye. He should be thankful to have this fleeting moment, but he was selfish and needed more. Time would forever be his enemy.

"I can remove your memories. You will soon forget the fear and pain you experienced. You can live hundreds, even thousands of lives without the torment you were forced to endure in this one."

"And you?" she asked as her pretty mouth twisted in a frown.

She snuggled into his warmth as he cupped her cheek. Damn love, if it only ended in heartbreak. Lucien stroked her tears away with the pad of his thumb.

"I'll remember for us both. I'll find you again and again, regardless of how many lives you live, Sadie. I'll ask you each time if you want me to remove your memories."

"Why?"

14

"It is the curse that's been placed upon us. When my heart beats again, I will find you. Until then, I will hunt Cain and Constance."

"I don't want that," she sobbed. "I want you."

"You'll always have me," he promised. "Even if you can't remember. I'll make you fall in love again and show you the beauty I found with you."

Her eyes met his dark ones. "You're crying."

"Am I?" He chuckled cynically.

His heart was breaking, but he couldn't tell her that. The cycle of goodbye tore him apart. She didn't realize it had been one hundred years since she died.

"So is this goodbye?" she sobbed.

"No, my love. We'll be together one day. I'll make you my queen and lay the ashes of our enemies at your feet."

"And what about you? Are you going to be all right?"

He shook his head and grinned with chagrin. "I just told you that your soul is doomed to Hell, and you're worried about me."

His Sadie. She would always be his, regardless of what circle of Hell she was in.

The smile on her face was broken as she coughed, and blood bubbled from her lips. Their time was cut short.

"I'm sorry, tulip," he said as tears rolled down his cheeks. "I'll bring our baby home and lay him in your arms. I love you, Sadie Winters."

"I love you, Luci—"

He cut her off by crashing his lips to hers in desperation for a last kiss, not wanting to rob either of them of that. The memory of her soft lips against his would sustain him in the darkest nights once his heart stopped beating.

She didn't need to know that he died every time she did. They were bound by blood, and their hearts beat as one. When one heart stopped, so did the other. When his heart beat again, he would know she had returned to a physical body.

"I will save you from this torment, no matter how long it takes."

———

LUCIFER WOULD NEVER FORGET the day Sadie died, as it haunted his every waking moment. Witnessing her anguish as she realized the fate that awaited her broke him. She screamed and tried to run on shaky legs.

He promised her he would find their child, and explained the deal he'd made to bring her soul back to life. She was doomed to a relentless cycle of Hell, and he was her captor, not her savior.

When he begged for one last kiss, she gave it freely. It was greedily accepted, like a man dying of thirst gulping water.

When their hearts stopped beating, the humanity Sadie'd awakened within him died as well.

He clung to her even when her body became cold and stiff, refusing to let her go. Had it been minutes, days, or weeks when he finally emerged from the snowy cocoon, giving her body to his mother?

The ice melted and buds returned to the trees, yet Lucifer remained on that mountainside, remiss to leave the spot where he'd last cradled his lover. The ground beneath his feet remained hardened. No life would ever return to that patch of doomed earth. And soon, the village would die as he had promised.

When he could no longer deny the fact she was gone, he tore the flesh from his bones once more. His eyes flooded with darkness as burning glyphs etched themselves into his skin. He sprouted horns that twisted like spirals and soon towered over the ground.

The sunny sky blackened with an oncoming storm as an ominous wind howled through the mountain air. Thunder clapped with Lucien's every footstep, and lightning flashed at the wave of his hand.

His first stop was tracking down Eliza Winters, Sadie's mother. The village folk screamed and ran as he drew near. Those he managed to catch had their minds invaded ruthlessly before he tossed their corpses aside. A trail of bodies followed him to the cottage.

The door splintered, and the woman inside shrieked. Her blonde hair and brown eyes reminded him of Beatrice.

He grabbed her and roared, "Where is Eliza?"

"Sh… she…" she shrieked and pointed to the anterior.

"Run."

It was the only act of mercy the demon was willing to offer, as he'd murdered her cousin for doing nothing more than attempting to help Sadie. With his debt paid, no other soul would survive the carnage. She stared wide-eyed, unsure where to go as he blocked the doorway. Lucifer stepped aside, and she ran, crying hysterically.

He wasn't in his right mind to offer her compensation, but she would never have to serve another person again. She would meet a wealthy merchant, and he would take care of her. She would be married within the year and bear multiple children.

He came across Eliza hiding in a closet. She screeched as he yanked her out by her golden curls. He hesitated for a moment when he saw the striking resemblance between her and the woman he loved.

"I condemn you to Hell for eternity, Eliza Winters."

His clawed hand tightened as she attempted to free herself from his grasp. He was unrelenting in his anger for retribution.

After being pulled from the home, she begged for mercy.

A low rumble sounded from his chest. "Did you show mercy to your daughter as you beat her for years? Did you show mercy when you sold her to a sadist?"

When she opened her mouth to retort, he grasped her tongue. With his superhuman strength, it took moments to tear the organ from its place.

Rumors were that royal servants had their tongues cut from their mouths. It wasn't true. They were controlled with memory manipulation. Brutal force was only necessary in certain circumstances, and Lucien was about to revel in it.

The woman's muffled sobs were ignored as he opened his maw and placed the bloody organ in his mouth. Though it was bitter and rubbery, his sharp teeth easily tore through it.

Lucifer swallowed it down with a wicked, bloody grin.

"Now your pathetic soul is mine to torment for eternity."

Never again would spiteful beratement roll off her tongue and hurt his Sadie—or anyone else.

He stalked closer to her once more, and she held her hands up as though he would halt. Lucifer grabbed her hand and crushed it in his fist, pulverizing every bone. Eliza's howls of pain were music to his ears. Torment and anguish were his lullaby.

He grasped her other wrist. Constance had made fun of Sadie's soft curves. But their mother was a large woman by comparison. Her daughter starved while she was well-fed.

Despite her corpulent size, he easily snapped the bone like a twig with a sharp crack. She screeched and blubbered, but he was far from finished.

"The pain she felt shall be yours tenfold."

He held up his razor-sharp claw and swiped it across her cheek. Blood mixed with the wetness and dripped onto her mud-stained gown.

He laughed as he threw her on her back. He stabbed his claw into her breast and sliced her open to her pubis. Lucifer dug his hands into the wound and tore her flesh apart.

Blood stained the packed dirt around her prone body. It always amazed him how much blood there was within a human body.

He destroyed layers of tissue and muscle; she wouldn't need them anymore. He wrapped his hand around her intestines and pulled. They threatened to slip from his grip, but he held firm. There was no hesitation, no stopping him now as he disemboweled his mother-in-law.

19

He had no rack nor animal to aid in the torture. But he relished in using his bare hands.

"Stay awake, bitch. I want you to remember this torment because you will relieve it every day for all eternity."

Souls were held prisoner in eternal damnation until their essence rotted away. Human imagination was solely responsible for images of Hell, and their sick nature conjured the torture that awaited them by demons.

As Eliza took her last breath, Lucifer began his wave of destruction. He mercilessly tore apart everyone until he heard the cry of a newborn. It wasn't his son; nonetheless, the child's cry turned him into a man once more.

He quickly found the crying child in the arms of Hilde, Sadie's friend. She held the infant close to her chest and begged, "Please spare him. He's my baby brother."

"All the innocent ones shall be spared, but no others."

"Bless you, m'lord," she cried.

He roared as she ran from the cottage. His skin erupted into flames, and he remained in the center of the burning village until the ashes scattered in the wind.

Constance

SOAKED in the blood of her sister and holding a wailing infant in her arms, Constance ran through the woods. Her blue gown, which matched her eyes, was stained an unnatural color. Her perfectly groomed hair was now unkempt, matching the wildness in her eyes.

Cain had instructed her to remove the child early to ensure its weakness. Its blood would've granted Constance immortality and allowed her to elevate to a member of The Society. But the slimy, deformed little thing took its first breath moments after being cut from Sadie's womb.

She hesitated, looking at its tiny horns and tail, and became startled when a servant gasped behind her. Constance immediately wrapped the baby in her cloak and absconded. In her haste, she dropped the dagger meant to pierce the child's heart.

A fresh snowfall began as they reached the tree line. Though her leather boots and cloak were designed to keep her warm, a chill ran down her spine. Wolves howled in the distance, making her painfully aware that she'd left her younger sister bleeding in the snow.

Constance shook the unwelcome guilt that threatened her out of her head. This was her chance to live more than her mundane existence, and there was no undoing what had been done.

When Cain approached their cottage and asked for Sadie, Constance became irate. What did her sister have that she didn't for the handsome lord? As the eldest, she was the beautiful one—the one bred for society. Her sister was a sow.

"I'll give anything to become The Winter Maiden," Constance blurted.

"Anything?" he asked with a devilish twinkle. "Even your sister's life?"

"Absolutely. She's your servant now. Do anything you want with her," Constance said without hesitation.

"What if I want you to serve me?" His lip quirked cloyingly.

"I don't serve anyone." Constance crossed her arms.

His eyes gazed over her curves hungrily.

"Do you know who I am?"

"Lord Cain."

He nodded and held her gaze for several minutes. When he finally broke eye contact, Constance felt dizzy. Cain casually crossed his arms and leaned against the doorframe.

"Do you know why our father skipped me and chose my younger brother?"

"No, my lord."

"Give me your sister, and I'll make your dreams come true."

———

WHEN SADIE SAUNTERED *up to the punch table at the Offering ball with a brilliant smile on her face, Constance's jealousy flared. When her sister declared she had been chosen as the Winter Maiden, that was the end of everything.*

After Lucien threatened her and kicked her out of the castle with the gold, she returned home to her mother.

"That wench was chosen by the prince. She stole my future!"

"You've returned with a dowry."

Constance turned toward her mother with a disgusted look. She picked up one of the gold coins and threw it back into the chest with a huff.

"The heifer's weight in gold. But that bitch will be bathed in luxury that should've been mine."

Eliza Winters shook her head and clicked her tongue. "With this money, we can buy you a new wardrobe. We'll purchase a carriage and move away. We'll hire a new servant, and you can be introduced into society. I'm sure we'll find a nobleman for you to marry."

"Lord Cain promised to elevate me, Mother. We only have to wait a few months."

———

EVEN THOUGH IT was winter on the mountain, the babbling brook remained unfrozen. The freezing water trickled down to the village where residents pulled fresh water from the spring. Constance dropped to her knees and unwrapped her cloak.

The baby blinked up at her with dark eyes. Its head was full of dark hair. The little cherub pout was all Sadie's. Constance had wanted to be the Winter Maiden but never wanted a child. She didn't want this one, either.

"My sister fucked up my entire life. Are you going to punish me now?" she mocked.

The baby's serpentine appendage coiled tightly around Constance's wrist. The very touch seared her skin with an intense, burning sensation. She could barely suppress a yelp at the agonizing pain.

With a mixture of panic and determination, she tried to pry the tail loose, but it was as if the baby's grip was made of steel. The tiny creature seemed to delight in the agony it inflicted as it tightened the coil.

As the seconds ticked by, Constance felt the heat of the tail penetrate her skin, leaving behind incinerated flesh. She needed to act quickly before the damage became irreversible.

In a desperate attempt to break free, Constance grabbed the baby's tail with her other hand and yanked with all her might to untangle it from her wrist and dropped the baby onto the bank.

"You fucking brat," she wheezed.

The baby's wails were deafening.

"Will you shut up!" Constance screeched at the wailing child.

The child's face contorted, and its skin cracked and became an inferno, burning Constance's hands and making her shriek. The tiny horn nubs grew longer, and the already dark eyes became pitch black.

Constance took the damned thing and thrust it beneath the surface of the icy spring water. Her heart beat wildly as hysterical laughter bubbled within her.

The child continued to thrash and wiggle as steamy vapor rose from the water's surface.

"What do we do now?" she hissed to the man standing over her shoulder.

"It's too late for the ritual. It's already found its demonic form. You can keep the child and raise it as your own."

The laughter broke free. The muscles in her cheeks hurt, and she thought she cracked a rib, as it hurt to breathe. Cain's hand cracked across her face, hard enough to make her vision go white. She greedily gasped for breath as she finally came back to her senses.

"Not the maternal type?" he asked with a mocking grin. "Even demons have mothers. Your sister gave birth to the one in your hands."

"Kill the little beast," Constance said. "Give me what you promised."

He became pensive for a moment. "My brother's spawn is strong. It infected the water with poison that would kill all the crops, livestock, and humans in the village with a plague.

Are you sure you don't want to witness the destruction this little one can bring firsthand?"

"I couldn't care less," she seethed.

"This child was destined to bring The Society out of the shadows and bridge the gap between our worlds. With the right nurturing of animosity, cruelty, and neglect, it will destroy the world. And you killed its mother."

"I don't care about this damn world as long as I get to spend eternity with you."

Constance's eyes widened in astonishment as she beheld a mesmerizing sight—the baby's skin was a vibrant hue of red, as though nature had imbued it with the essence of flora, giving it an ethereal glow. Little droplets of water quickly evaporated off its burning skin.

"What do we do now?"

"Give me the child, Constance."

Lucifer

BEING adrift in a torrent of emotions paralyzed Lucien. He returned to Hell to see his father.

Satan's castle rose in the heart of a desolate landscape, atop an active volcano, seeming to taunt the very force of nature, daring it to erupt. Long, dark spires twisted and reached toward the heavens, reminiscent of a demon's horns. These spires were not mere architectural embellishments but a manifestation of the malevolence that dwelt within the castle.

The walls, forged from obsidian, stood as an impenetrable barrier, reflecting the fiery glow of the lava. The obsidian's smooth, jet-black surface held seeds of evil within its walls.

The castle was a place where darkness thrived, and hope withered away. Lucifer was home for the first time in centuries.

Though he had wings, Lucifer climbed the steps leading to the castle. His heart no longer beat, but if it did, it would tap out a fierce rhythm as though he were about to face impending doom.

"Welcome home, young master." The underworld creature bowed to him as he entered.

Aside from demons and tortured souls, there were many castes of creatures and other beings in Hell.

His father's advisors possessed serpentine bodies that slithered with eerie grace, while their humanoid features made them ghastly.

They possessed a deep-seated knowledge of the arcane secrets and intricacies of Hell. They understood the dark mysteries of the underworld and how to harness the dark powers.

They had taught Lucifer how to disguise himself in human form and how to call upon his demonic self as needed. They taught him how to harness his powers over the element of fire, which connected him to the magma of his home.

The loyalty of these creatures was unwavering as they carried out their tasks with a sense of devotion that bordered on fanaticism. From time to time, one of the creatures would escape the bowels of Hell and appear among the mortals. They sowed discord like any minion of Hell, except they drew mortals into satanic worship.

In doing this, they were quickly caught by demons who recognized their brutish nature and lack of subtlety. They swiftly dispatched the lower creatures and sent them to oblivion, a void where everything ceased to exist.

Creatures were indispensable assets and used as pawns in grander schemes to seize power and influence.

"I'm here to see, Satan," Lucifer said.

"Of course, Your Highness," it hissed.

Lucifer's wings folded against his back, their gray feathers remaining dull in the dim light of the corridor. His footsteps were silent as he walked with regal grace against the floor.

The air was heavy with anticipation as they neared the throne room. His mood dampened with animosity like a storm gathering strength.

Satan's aura encompassed the entirety of the castle, making every being within its walls hyper-aware of the subtlest shift in his mood. Lucifer's senses were on alert.

He paused and took a deep breath before the grand doors. A confrontation between father and son was inevitable.

———————

"IT IS time for you to sire an heir, Lucifer."

Lucifer had been summoned to Satan's throne. The air crackled with electricity as father and son stared at one another. There were no similarities in their human forms as it was the demonic form that father passed to son.

The only feature they had in common was the darkened eyes that all demons possessed. They burned with an otherworldly intensity as they came face-to-face. Lucifer's eyes blazed with a mixture of defiance and pride, reflecting the inner turmoil that consumed him.

"No," he said firmly.

Satan's armor clanged as he stood. The man was dressed in heavy metal to protect his body at all times. It had been a millennium since the last insurgence rose and culminated in an attempt at his life, but he refused to give a lesser demon the chance to strike him down again.

The demon's presence commanded respect and fear in equal measure, his very essence embodying unyielding darkness. There was no room for sentimentality or compassion in him. The angelic side of Lucifer was treated as a defect.

His father often attempted to beat the good out of his son. Lucifer had been left with many broken bones; sometimes he would be knocked unconscious for days. He had been thrown into the mouth of the volcano and swallowed by magma.

Though the flesh melted from his bones in an instant, the excruciating agony lingered. He was reduced to nothingness and resurrected only to face the same fate repeatedly. This torment went on until he learned to stop screaming from the torment of regeneration and threw himself voluntarily into the angry abyss.

The smell of sulfur was imbued within his skin. The demons cheered at the destruction of the good in him. Not only did they watch as his wings burned in the lava, but they would pluck the feathers out of him the moment they grew back.

Lucifer was full of hatred when he stared at his father in defiance. His rebellious spirit refused to bow in Satan's formidable presence. He didn't give a shit about his father's demands. He would sire no heir.

"Let my brother do it."

Cain was shrouded in darkness and tormented by his jealousy long before Lucifer was born. He killed his twin brother, Abel, due to the festering, deep-seated envy that blackened his soul. It was after this that Cain was welcomed into Hell as Satan's son.

The wretchedness of Cain's bitter resentment continued to grow. When Lucifer was sent to his father's side in Hell, the brothers became rivals. The torture and torment that Lucifer endured at the hands of demonic forces were a testament to the depths of his brother's hatred.

Satan encouraged this rivalry between his sons. He nurtured the festering wounds left behind until he sent them to the surface world of mortals. Cain was a true harbinger, harvesting multitudes of souls for his father, while Lucifer spent his time in solitude.

Yes, Lucifer indulged in pleasures of the flesh, plucking an errant soul occasionally, but he didn't relish in it like his brother. Lucifer searched for meaning in his bleak existence.

The profound question that echoed through his heart remained with him: Did the absence of love between father and sons truly matter? Why was he desperate to find meaning and validation in a world without affection?

Cain's story should serve as a cautionary tale regarding the power of jealousy and the lengths one might go in pursuit of recognition. His black heart was far better suited to ruling those in Hell, not Lucifer.

"It is not for you to defy my will. The oracle has seen your future. Your son will bring demons out of the shadows and usher in a new era for Hell."

Lucifer had never entertained the notion of siring a child before. Demon males lay with innocent maidens and poisoned their wombs with their seed. In most cases, the mothers didn't survive birth as the tiny demons clawed their way out of the birth canal.

In Lucifer's case, since he was part angel, only a specific type of soul could bear his heir. She had to be pure of heart, soul, and body. His child would be born part demon, but mostly pure and innocent.

For the first time in a long time, Lucifer thought of the angelic part of himself. His mother had been one of those pure souls and ascended to gain her wings. Would the woman he sired a child with do the same?

It was a path Lucifer never envisioned. Yet when he imagined a tiny child in his arms, he couldn't help but feel a foreign surge of emotion. He had never known love or tenderness, but he was willing to offer it. He was willing to protect and nurture his child even though he had no idea what it took to guide an innocent soul through the corrupt world.

Sadie

AMIDST THE VAST expanse of the tundra, Sadie couldn't stay warm. She stood as still as a crystalline sculpture, naked and covered with a layer of salt. Her skin glistened under the pale hue of a foreign body of light.

Her long hair was twisted into icy tendrils, forming a frigid crown atop her head. Her stark beauty cracked in the unforgiving elements. She'd never experienced a harsher winter before. The frozen landscape promised to hold her forever.

The frozen lake stretched as far as the eye could see. Many people, like her, stood on a patch of ice, praying their patch wouldn't crack beneath their feet.

Eerie shadowy beings glided along the glossy surface. Their presence sent shivers down Sadie's spine. She held her breath whenever they turned in her direction. When the world plunged into darkness, the shadows howled in a spine-chilling symphony. As if possessed by an unseen force, they would lunge at their chosen victims, pull their bodies below the surface, and drown them in the freezing water.

The frigid waters swallowed their victims, enveloping them in a merciless embrace. When the artificial sun rose again, they would see the tormented faces of those who disappeared the night before.

This cycle continued for seven days before Sadie's hair was brushed aside by one of the beings. She bit her lip to suppress a shriek. It was her turn. Spectral hands caressed her shoulders and whispered unintelligible words against the shell of her ear.

Sadie's thoughts drifted to Lucien and the consuming love she'd experienced. She found solace in the memories they shared, and the fleeting moments of bliss.

Fate had been unkind, tearing them apart before they could live a happy life together. Sobs wracked her body at her one regret—not being able to hold her child.

She wept, unable to face her demise with dignity in the face of the inevitable. Sadie closed her eyes, refusing to let fear consume her in her final moments. Instead, she focused once more on Lucien. She remembered the warmth in his arms and the sulfur scent that was all his.

The name of her lover was a whisper on her lips. "Lucien."

The creature howled, and the ice cracked beneath Sadie's feet. A hand grasped her ankle and pulled her through the ice. Love would transcend the boundary between life and death.

Sadie's lungs froze as she drifted into the unknown. She couldn't see or hear anything in the dark void.

Fight.

In the shadowy depths, Sadie's survival instinct awakened as an unseen force wrapped around her ankle. Panic surged through her, and desperation fueled her movements. With every ounce of strength she could muster, Sadie thrashed and kicked in an attempt to break free from the ruthless grip.

Her lungs burned with the need to breathe. They pleaded for air as the depths threatened to claim her.

She clawed her way upward until her head finally broke the still surface of the water. The icy lake had turned into a calm stream. Sadie climbed out onto the grassy bank and collapsed, gasping and coughing, greedily gulping precious air.

She closed her eyes, willing her body to stop trembling. She gasped and clutched her chest, feeling her heart that had been quiet race furiously.

Exhausted, she fell asleep.

SADIE AWAKENED ALONE in a dark alley. Her naked body was covered in soot and grime. Her hair was matted, and her scalp itched as though infested with bugs.

Her throat was parched, and she was desperate for a fresh water source, but the stream she had fallen asleep near was no longer there.

In her search, she stumbled upon a macabre sight.

She had to walk around a large patch of dirt where people's feet pushed up from the ground like a field of daisies. However, instead of a colorful array of flowers being kissed by the sun and touched by a gentle breeze, the feet were blackened as several dragons breathed fire on one pair of feet before going to the next, down a long line as far as the eye could see.

In her haste to leave, she slammed into a person's chest. When she looked up to apologize, she gasped in terror. She was staring at the back of the person's head. She jumped to the side, and the person's face was grotesque and twisted. Hair hung from its gaping mouth and nostrils. The eyes focused on nothing. If they experienced agony, she couldn't tell. But how could one not?

Sadie heard rushing water and ran toward it. Unfortunately, she was mistaken. The disgusting smell of human excrement offended her nose. She quickly raised her hand in an attempt to cover the foul stench and watched in horror as people fought the current. Nausea bubbled up in her alongside hysteria.

Demons held whips or their tails in hand and hit people's backsides. Sadie remembered the painful kiss against her back. The cries of those being whipped were nearly drowned out by the gleeful squeals of those inflicting the punishment. One demon raised its head and winked with a wicked grin. She shook her head and stepped back.

A black bubbling substance spouted from a geyser, like a fountain in a center square. A tight ring of bodies standing shoulder-to-shoulder watched as one after the other was picked up and tossed into the geyser. Their shrieking was quickly silenced as the tar enveloped their entire body. A few of the people were pulled out and had feathers dumped over them. No matter how many people were pulled from the ring, it remained a tight circle of bodies.

She finally saw people clothed in robes. Though she wasn't Christian, she recognized the vestments as belonging to those in the Church. Sadie shook as one of them approached her. His skeletal hand trembled as it fought the weight of the garment, reaching for her. She held her breath, and a moment before it grasped her, the arm fell. She exhaled in relief.

Snakes slithered this way and that across the ground, but they seemed to be headed in one direction. Why Sadie followed them, she couldn't say for sure. She watched in horror as a snake climbed a person's legs and coiled around their wrists, binding the person's hands behind their back. Another snake bit into the man's penis. But instead of sounds of agony, he sounded pleasured. He was bent over by the demon behind him whose appendage was large like a stallion. Sadie placed her hand over her mouth to stifle a gasp as he thrust into the man.

Someone slammed into her back, and she tumbled to the ground. Sadie knew she was in trouble if she remained there so did her best to get back on her feet, but another blow from behind had her face in the dirt. Panic clawed at her throat as the dirt turned to snow around her.

She screamed and rolled over, kicking wildly at the one who had knocked her down. Her eyes widened in horror as tongues of fire licked across his skin. There was no source for the flames that engulfed the person's body. The scent of burning flesh choked Sadie as she watched the person's flesh melt from their bones and reduce to a pile of ash before her.

Her breasts swayed as she scooched away from another being coming toward her. She scrambled to her feet and hurried away.

She came upon another circle of humans. They wore heavy collars that were connected by chains to a large wooden spike in the middle. They had slowly walked in the circle so long that they had sunk into the ground to their ankles. Many people were missing limbs; a couple even walked without heads. They reminded her of cattle headed to slaughter. Demons wielding machetes circled them and at random would chop off a head or limb. The wounds seemed to heal quickly; several had limbs in states of regeneration, only for the demons to chop it off again.

She stumbled upon a group of people seeming to suffer some sort of plague or leprosy. Their skin had various oozing wounds full of writhing maggots and festering boils. They scratched themselves until their skin bled. Hair fell out in clumps, leaving large bald spots on their bodies. They wailed for water from a never-ending thirst.

Sadie's throat burned as she watched. She needed to find a source of water.

She gasped and fell to her knees as her heart began beating furiously. It was a foreign feeling to her in the darkness. Every eye trained on her. Humans and demons alike took step after step in her direction. Her heart became wild as it pushed adrenaline through her veins.

"Please," she begged. "Don't."

There was no path to escape as she was encircled. A scream tore from Sadie's dry throat as the first person reached her. Just before it grasped her, she was pulled away by an invisible force.

Constance

"WHERE ARE WE?" Constance asked.

"Welcome to Hell, my dear." Cain breathed in deeply. "The acrid scent of death and decay—I love it."

A suffocating heaviness weighed on Constance's heart. It was a burden unlike any other. A myriad of emotions swirled within her, causing a tumultuous storm. She was overwhelmed with sorrow and grief, but for what, she didn't know. Disappointment at missed opportunities and gnawing guilt ate at her.

Her envy cast a mirror into her blackened heart. Her soul shriveled with the sins she had committed against her sister and the baby. The lengths to which Constance had gone to achieve her own selfish goals carried insurmountable consequences. Only now, awareness of such wickedness was hers.

Each emotion pressed upon her spirit and cast a shadow over her life. She felt the pressure to succeed, to live up to the beauty standards set by society and her mother. The pressure had been relentless, a constant reminder of her inadequacies and the fear of failure. Would things have been different if she weren't the firstborn Winters child? Whether expectations were real or imagined no longer mattered.

Constance yearned for release. She longed to unburden herself, and the first step was getting rid of the brat in her arms. She longed to cast it aside into the mist and be free of this trap.

As Constance grappled with the heaviness of her heart, she knew there was no turning back. She'd walked this path alone long before Cain tempted her. She'd willingly made a bargain with him, and now it was time to face the consequences.

They were in a field of nothingness. The atmosphere was gloomy and dimly lit. Occasionally they wandered across clumps of gnarled trees. Hundreds of faces were frozen in agony within the bark.

Souls wandered aimlessly. They neither heard nor saw nor paid attention to Constance, Cain, and the tiny infant.

"Where are we?" Constance asked again.

"We are in limbo, or as Catholics call it, purgatory."

"Why are we here?"

"This is where the child will spend eternity. In limbo, it will not grow or change."

Constance glanced down at the sleeping baby in her arms. When she pulled it free from the stream, it had screamed and wailed until it fell asleep. The horns on its head had sunk back into the soft skull, and its tail fell off and withered like a husk.

"The tail will return," Cain explained.

He explained demonic anatomy in a crash course. "Demons have multiple forms. You've only seen my glimmer, or human guise, if you will. This is the form I use to tempt mortals, as I appear alluring and seductive."

He caressed Constance's cheek, which caused a shiver of delight to shoot down her spine. Cain chuckled as it proved his point.

"Lesser demons are ugly. They require blood to sustain their youthful glow." He pointed to the sleeping infant. "Lower demons who fornicate and impregnate humans produce spawn that will not survive anyway. They drink their blood to sustain themselves.

"Demons of my caliber can change form at will. My demonic form is powerful and is only sated with a human sacrifice. My brother is a freak and has an angelic form as well. My mother was mortal; therefore, I do not have this third form."

"Do you think the baby has an angelic form too?" Constance asked in awe.

"I doubt it, as only its demonic form was awakened. Believe me, we don't want it to assume an angelic form. Otherwise, it can't stay in limbo, and we need it here."

Constance tried to remember what the Church said about purgatory. They weren't Catholic or Christian, but a lot of the villagers followed this new faith, including their father, once a church had been erected in the village.

They constantly preached that absolution was the way to Heaven, and practically everything else was a ticket to Hell. There was no doubt in Constance's mind where she would end up. But seeing Hell outside of a religious construct wasn't what she imagined it to be or what the church leaders promised.

She wanted to laugh at the lack of the Lord's mercy. *The Lord works in mysterious ways* was whispered in their mother's ear often when their father was sick and even after he passed away. If He existed, He surely wasn't there for her sister.

"What will happen to the baby here?"

Cain laughed. "Don't tell me your sense of noble obligation has suddenly awakened because of a little beast."

Emotion bubbled again within her. When she had pulled the tiny creature from her sister's body, it fought for breath. When she threatened it, it fought back, leaving a nasty, painful burn on her wrist. Even though she tried to drown the child, its will to live superseded everything, and it calmed once the threat to its life passed. She couldn't help but admire its survival instinct.

"*Cain*," she hissed.

"The souls in limbo aren't punished or tortured like they are in the other circles of Hell. There are no illusions or games here. What you see—" He gestured around them. "—is what you get. The child isn't old enough to understand where it is. Those that blindly wander know there is an upper world, the one Christians call Heaven." He spat. "And they know they are denied entry. Those trapped here are those who have not committed intentional sins during life. They remain here for centuries before they are judged. They are either reborn, sent above, or sent below."

Constance nodded in an attempt to digest the complexity of Cain's explanations.

"Will my sister come here?"

Cain's laughter filled the entirety of the void they were in. The dull eyes of the souls around them turned toward them. Constance's skin crawled as they stepped closer. The closer they came, the higher her anxiety climbed. Her throat closed, and her lungs felt as though the oxygen was being squeezed out of them.

The baby was plucked from her arms as she dropped to her knees.

"Give it back!" she screamed as the baby wailed.

The vibrant red of the child's skin was drained in a second. Twisted horns grew from its head once more, and its tail sliced through the air like a whip.

The soul that had grabbed the infant disappeared in a puff like a cloud. Its anguished cry filled the space just as Cain's laughter had, and all the souls within the immediate vicinity exploded similarly.

"It doesn't need protection," Cain chuckled. "It is a higher-level demon."

"What about my sister?"

"Your sister will never ascend nor will she come to limbo. She willingly fornicated with the son of Satan. She bound her soul to my brother. She will experience Hell at its finest." His lips curled in a wicked smile. "You promised her to me. She will be mine."

Envy tore through Constance at an alarming rate. Even in death, Cain chose *her*.

"What does she have that I don't?" she asked shrilly.

Cristina Lollabrigida

Cain grabbed her chin in a bruising grip. "I live in Hell. I've fucked many skilled succubi. There are millions of dark souls willing to fall on their knees and beg for my cock. I've laid with thousands of humans. I can easily seduce any maiden out of her clothing and convince her to climb onto all fours in the middle of a field and scream as I bury myself inside her. Pure souls like your sister's aren't seen often. I crave to make a sinner out of her."

Lucifer

"YOU RULE HELL. How can you not find my son?"

Lucifer hardly kept his wrath in check. His hands were clenched into fists so tight that the skin turned white. Tension coiled inside of him as the veins on his neck and forearms bulged, threatening to burst from his skin.

Satan refused to let Sadie free from the depths of Hell unless Lucifer agreed to take his throne title as Prince of Hell. He had no choice if he was to save the woman he loved. She was the only thing that made him willing to make such a sacrifice.

Lucien's unyielding determination and devotion to Sadie would only break her heart. Being stuck on his throne meant he would never see her again.

Their only option to be together was to pull her out of Hell himself. But he couldn't do that until he had their child. He wouldn't leave Hell without his son.

He felt the faint heartbeat within his soul; the subtle rhythm was the only link he had to his child. It had been hundreds of years, and he had failed to keep his promise to Sadie.

His brother and Constance continued to jump from Earth to Hell and back again. The remaining fragments of his hopes and dreams fell apart. The delicate balance he had walked for so long was exhausting.

Each time he bid farewell to Sadie, a piece of his soul shattered. Every goodbye kiss lingered on his lips despite the heavy toll on his body. He was plunged into a state of profound melancholy, which threw him into a murderous rage. The goodness within him eroded as though crashing waves continued to toss him against a rocky shore.

The ominous clanking of the metal on Satan's armor echoed through the chamber as he stepped toward Lucifer. Each footfall sent a thunderous rumble against the cold stone floor. Despite the intimidating display, Lucifer stood still, refusing to flinch, as he had anticipated his father's reaction. Satan raised his fist and delivered a blow with the force of his darkness behind it.

Lucifer sailed across the room and slammed into the obsidian wall. He roared as the phantom shadows encircled his limbs and held him against the wall. Lucifer's strength was nothing compared to his father's, as Satan's throne fed him the powers of the underworld.

"Before you ascend your throne, I will destroy the sentimentality within you."

CAIN STROLLED into the throne room, dragging a naked and restrained Sadie along with him. Lucifer's eyes went wide at the black rings coiled around her neck and the snacks that encircled her wrists.

"Let her go," he snarled.

"As if you're in a place to tell me how to handle my prize."

Cain grinned wickedly as he yanked the chain hard enough that she stumbled over her bare feet. With her bound hands, she couldn't brace her fall. She cried out as her knees hit the stone floor.

"Sadie!" Lucifer bellowed, struggling against his bonds.

"Quiet, or I will gag you," Satan commanded.

"Touch her, and I will fucking tear you apart, Cain. I will dismember you and scatter your parts to every realm of Hell," he promised.

Satan waved his hand, and the darkness entered Lucien's mouth. He continued to thrash as Cain stroked Sadie's cheek before smacking her so hard she fell over. Her whimpers filled the chamber. Lucifer's soul was set ablaze.

"Father invited me to provide entertainment as you ascend your throne."

Cain roared as he turned his body inside out. His jet-black horns didn't twist like Lucifer's; instead, they conformed to the shape of his head as though slicked back. His forked tail swung slowly from side to side. His body didn't glow in ethereal glyphs, but the etchings against his dark skin looked like his body burned from the inside out.

He approached the fallen Sadie and whipped her cheek with his tail, slicing it open. Blood trickled down her cheek, reminding Lucifer of the first time he saw her on the lane hundreds of years before. Would she forgive him for standing aside as his brother assaulted her again?

Sadie yelped as Cain's tail whipped her ass. No one had the right to make her cry. The bands around Lucifer suppressed his powers, but his fury bubbled beneath the surface. Any more, and he would erupt like the volcano the castle stood upon.

Cain clawed at Sadie's plump breasts and flicked his tongue against her buds. His lips trailed down her soft stomach, burning her skin. She shrieked as he bit into her hip, tearing into her flesh like an animal. He dug into her wound with his finger and used the blood to circle between her thighs.

Lucifer watched in horror as his brother positioned Sadie on all fours, facing him, and positioned himself behind her. She screamed as he thrust himself inside her. He yanked her hair and forced her head up. Her eyes were closed, so he couldn't communicate with her, but his brother's dark eyes were full of mockery.

"I fucked her like this every day for months after you left her. Nothing about her was innocent anymore."

When Satan pulled his eldest son away from Sadie, he picked her up and forced her to sink on his cock. Sadie whimpered as he snapped his hips furiously, almost tearing her apart.

"I see how you fell for this one. Her cunt is squeezing my cock like a sleeve. How many loads do you think she could handle?"

The air around Lucifer trembled as his eyes blazed with a hellish intensity. His power erupted like a cataclysmic eruption, shaking the foundation of the dark castle. He twisted in unbridled and wild rage. The chains that held him were obliterated. Liquid fire ran through his veins as a thunderous roar broke free from his chest.

The powers of Hell might belong to his father, but he had angelic powers within him. His desire to save Sadie was stronger than his desire to kill his father and brother, and that set him free. In that moment, he became a force of nature that couldn't be stopped.

"Let her go!" His powerful bellow cracked the stone walls around him.

His father and brother stepped away from the weeping woman. Lucifer wrapped her in his arms, only to discover she wasn't Sadie. She was a succubus in disguise.

Lucifer's heart began to beat.

Sadie

LOST and wet in a squelching swamp, Sadie was overcome by a fit of rage. She dashed through the murky water surrounding her ankles in an attempt to evade the souls trying to engage her in combat.

Some souls donned armor and held swords or spears. Sadie watched as the weapons clashed and those who lost limbs screamed in agony. The death rattles never ceased.

She snuck around and picked up a short sword. It was heavier than she imagined it would be. But she rolled her shoulders and held firmly onto the handle. Sadie screamed as she pierced the gut of a demon who lunged at her.

"Leave me alone!" she screamed at the laughing creature.

"Embrace your fate, Sadie Winters," it hissed. "You hide your nature well, but you are the darkest soul here."

"That's not true!" she cried.

"But it issss…"

"Die!"

No matter how many times she drove her sword through the belly of the demon, it wouldn't die. It laughed maniacally and continued to taunt her.

Sadie tore her hair out as she howled in rage. She blinked and was suddenly confronted with a mirror image of herself. A sense of foreboding washed over her as their eyes locked.

Her gaze dropped to the doppelgänger's mouth. Its crimson lips twisted into a grotesque smile. Sadie was trapped in a nightmare as her reflection warped into something sinister.

Blood bubbled and oozed from the corners of her mouth as she laughed hysterically. Sadie trembled as she fought the urge to flee the face-off. The metallic scent of blood mingled with the mossy stench of the swamp.

As Sadie stared into the black soulless eyes, a chill ran down her spine. She realized a heartbeat too late that she'd let her guard down. However, before she was struck down, an invisible force carried her away.

SADIE JOLTED UPRIGHT IN BED, her heart pounded against her ribcage. The sweat-drenched sheets tangled around her legs and clung to her skin. She struggled to shake off the twisted nightmares she was plagued with.

The firelight cast dancing shadows on the stone walls, neither mocking nor cheering her up. Her hands trembled as she pushed the sheets off her body. She tried to calm her racing heart and mind.

Lucien's breathing remained steady next to her as he rested in slumber. She looked down at his naked back and brushed his hair from his forehead. He made a contented sound but didn't awaken.

Sadie pushed all thoughts from her mind and placed a kiss on her lover's shoulder, then trailed kisses along his spine. Since sleep wouldn't find her again, she wanted to find comfort in his embrace. Lucien was the remedy for her lingering fears. He gave her the courage to face the darkness that haunted her.

"You're up early," he grumbled in a scratchy voice.

"I'm sorry I woke you," she said with a smile, not feeling the slightest bit apologetic.

"What's on your mind?"

He gave Sadie a quick peck on the lips as she wrapped her arms around his shoulders.

"I was hoping we could bathe in the creek today and then visit Hilde. It's been so long."

A flicker of emotion flashed across Lucien's face before he rewarded her with a smile. Sadie's longing gaze flicked in the direction of the window where the heavy curtain obscured the early morning light.

"You don't need to bathe in the creek, tulip. I can have the servants draw a warm bath for us. After we're finished, we'll go for a walk."

While not a skilled swimmer as many of the common folk, Sadie found joy in the refreshing, cool waters of the creek. On hot summer days, the youngest children in the village stripped their clothing and splashed in the shallows. Men and maidens, like her, wore their underclothes to shield their nakedness as they bathed in the creek. However, when they emerged from the waters, their soaked clothes clung like a second skin, not offering much modesty.

The priest referred to this behavior as sinful, shaming young men and women and preaching that they shouldn't enjoy such dalliances outside of their marital beds. That didn't stop them from wading in the shallows and letting the gentle current wash over their feet.

Sadie loved the way the sunlight danced on the surface of the water. She and Hilde would often lie on the banks, sunning themselves and watching the clouds drift lazily overhead. They would giggle and point out the various shapes they saw in the sky. On cloudless days, they shared village gossip and their dreams for the future.

Those innocent days by the creek brought joy and a wave of sadness, as they felt so far away now. She sighed, not being able to hide her melancholy from her lover. Lucien lifted her hand and kissed her palm.

"Let's go to the creek," he said.

Her face brightened and she shrieked gleefully. "Oh, Lucien. Thank you!"

Sadie stretched with cat-like grace before rolling out of bed and grabbing Lucien's hand. She playfully tugged him after her with a mischievous grin. He laughed, and a rare glimmer of lightheartedness flickered in his eyes.

Her heart beat in pure joy. Every moment with Lucien felt like an eternity of bliss. She sank into his warmth as he cupped her cheek. After the nightmare that had awoken her, this moment felt like a dream she never wanted to wake from.

Their hands remained intertwined as they emerged from the castle. Sadie's spirits soared like a bird taking flight as the sun's rays kissed her skin.

Spring was one of her favorite seasons, as nature awakened from her winter slumber. The grass was lush and a vibrant green, while the trees budded. Birds perched on branches, chirping and warbling happy songs.

Eventually, the creek came into view. Its gentle burbling welcomed them as the glossy surface reflected the picturesque sky. They were able to enjoy the morning in solitude.

"Come here, Sadie."

Lucien wrapped his arms around her waist and pulled her against him, and she wrapped her arms around his neck.

"I love you, Sadie Winters," he said against her lips.

"Lucien—" she whispered.

He didn't allow her to finish her response before pressing his lips against hers. While she loved hearing him profess his feelings—words were never necessary. He'd trusted her with his deepest secrets long ago, and their souls were intertwined. In the moment of silent connection, their hearts beat as one.

"Make love to me. Please."

"You never have to ask."

Lucien's nimble fingers untied the silk ribbons of Sadie's fur-trimmed cloak. He undid the lacing on the bodice of her gown and slid it from her shoulders. His lips warmed every spot of her pale skin as it was bared, leaving goosebumps in their wake. He peppered kisses along her collar and full breasts.

Sadie's head fell back with a soft moan. Something was so familiar in the way her body craved his touch, but subconsciously, she knew how much she'd missed it, as though it had been so long since the last time they were together.

She shook the intrusive thought from her mind and focused on the sensation of Lucien's touch as his hand slid between her thick thighs.

"Your body is beautiful, tulip. I love your soft skin and rounded curves. Your breasts are a perfect handful, and your ass is like a succulent peach."

Lucien spoke against her skin as his gentle touch became bolder and his kisses more ardent. When he sucked on her neck hard enough to leave a mark, she gasped.

"What's gotten into you?"

"I want you to bear my marks, Sadie. I want the world to see you belong to me."

The desperation in his voice gave her pause. She wanted love, but he seemed to need more. They were soulmates, and nothing they did together was wrong. His unwavering devotion was enough for her.

"I remember you once told me there were different ways to make love. Will you show me what you want?"

She spoke quickly out of embarrassment, trying to convey her thoughts. A flush pinked her skin, and Sadie hid behind a curtain of her dark hair.

The rumble of laughter from Lucien's chest turned her from pink to scarlet. He put his fingers beneath her chin and forced her to look up at him.

"Don't hide from me, little succubus."

She squeaked as he lifted her naked body and carried her over to a birch tree.

"Grab onto the trunk, Sadie."

Her mouth formed a wordless o as she watched wide-eyed as he reached for a bough and snapped it from the tree. He grabbed the ends and flexed it slightly before waving it before him, testing its flexibility. Sadie trembled as he brushed her bare back with his fingertips.

"I'm not going to whip your back with the switch, tulip. I'm going to use this on your ass."

"Why?" she asked.

Without responding, he whipped her behind, causing her to yelp. He did it again immediately, not giving her a chance to recover from the first sting. He did it multiple times before approaching her and massaging the sore globes with his hand. The deliciously painful sting mixed with the rush of blood and his tender touch caused her core to become slick with desire.

"How does that feel?" he asked against the shell of her ear.

Though his penis was still in the confines of his breeches, she felt the power of it pressed against her hip. He pinched her nipple and rolled it between his thumb and forefinger. Pain and pleasure tendrils coiled within her making her shaky with desire.

"I need more, Lucien," she mewed.

"Keep your hands on the tree," he instructed.

He teased her with kisses down her spine until he bit her ass cheek. His fingertips gently ran up her arms, but then he grasped a fistful of her hair and yanked just enough for her to feel a tingle in her scalp.

"Lucien... please..." she begged.

His hand slipped over her mouth, and he growled, "This is what I want, tulip. I need you to be as desperate as I fucking am. I want you painfully aroused by my seduction and willing to sell your soul for a taste of my cock. Nod if you understand."

Her breath quickened as her chest rose and fell. They were already bound by heart, body, and soul. Yet, she would willingly give him every bit of herself if that was what he needed. She squealed beneath his hand as he yanked her hair again.

"I said, nod if you understand."

It was better not to provoke the beast within him, and she nodded.

"Good little tulip. I remember how you tried to dismiss me the first time. You wanted to treat this as transactional. But I knew I was going to keep you for my eternity. Fuck, Sadie, I'll never have enough of these little moments."

Tears welled in Sadie's eyes as his words struck a chord within her. It was what he didn't say that caused his voice to waiver and why he forced her to look away from him.

He slid himself between her thighs and parted her lips. His thick cock probed her entrance. She cried out as he thrust into her with a single stroke. She'd taken him many times before, but this time, they both wanted it to hurt.

There was no starting slow. Lucien's hands gripped her hips, leaving half-moon impressions on her skin. Her hands slipped on the smooth bark as Lucien pistoned in and out of her at a furious pace. Her breasts swayed back and forth as his hips slapping against hers added to the cacophony of her cries.

"Take it for me. Fuck me. Love me."

"I will... I do..."

Cain

THE AIR WAS CHARGED with anticipation as Cain and
Constance approached the legendary seer. He could sense
Constance's heart pounding furiously as she stepped closer to
the decrepit old woman.

"I am not old," the woman said in a craggy voice. "I am the
universe."

As she turned toward them, they saw that her eyes were
covered with a milky film.

"You're blind!" Constance gasped. "Our neighbor's cat gave
birth to a kitten with milky white eyes once. My father
drowned it in the creek saying it was more humane than
allowing it to suffer."

"I am not blind, child. I see everything. I know why you've
come to see me."

"Revered seer," Cain began. "I have come to you with a
conundrum."

"I know why you've come to see me," she hissed. "What I want is to see the woman."

As Constance approached the revered oracle, the woman held out her hand, causing her to recoil. Her eyes bore into Constance's soul while observing every plain of existence, peering into the very fabric of time.

She cackled "You have no *destiny* here, child. Heavy hands will judge you once every last coin is spent. Your womb has been cursed, but you have become a mother. Your future is shrouded in mystery with many choices that will weigh over your veil."

The weight of uncertainty hung in the air as the oracle let go of Constance's hand. Though cryptic, the oracle's words set in motion a chain of events that would shape the course of Constance's future.

The Seer turned her attention toward Cain. She took several slow steps toward him and bowed deeply. When she raised her eyes to his, he felt an invisible force pulling him into her realm. The air crackled with energy, which battered him. His demonic form threatened to erupt.

"None of that now, young master. I know why you're here. You've been desperate to achieve, but you'll never receive recognition. You thirst for pleasure you can never experience. Nothing will sate your hunger. Her affections are not a prize to be won. Your nature doesn't allow you another path, but if it did, you would find fulfillment."

Her words angered him, and his face twisted in a grimace. "Don't speak to me in ridiculous riddles. Tell me what I need to know."

She held her hand toward Constance. "Where is my payment?"

Cain yanked Constance's cloak open. His brother's child was asleep, nestled against her breast.

"You've become a mother." She smiled.

Constance's eyes went wide. "That's not true. I'm not a mother. It didn't deserve to be left in purgatory."

The crone nodded thoughtfully. "Give me the child."

Constance hesitated, glancing down at the sleeping baby. Cain clicked his tongue in annoyance. She reluctantly handed the tiny bundle over to the woman's withered hands.

"You can't take the child to the world of mortals, either, not without its mother."

"Satan had five children—did you know? His eldest was a daughter. She was kind-hearted and beautiful, and the only one who made her father smile. One birthday he promised to give her whatever her heart desired. She wished for a single flower, but not just any flower. She wanted one that would bring joy not to herself or her father, but to mortals. She wanted to plant them and bring a single one home with her. What else could a proud father do but honor his daughter's selfless wish? She went to the land of mortals with no disguise, as she'd never had to hide her nature before. Unfortunately, she learned the wickedness of man. They bound her body, forced themselves upon her, and murdered her. They cut her body into pieces, burned her, and scattered her ashes among their fields. Even in death, her nature was gentle. She fertilized the fields, and that's where roses come from.

"The second born was a son. This child was the exact opposite of his sister. He was angry and often lashed out in violent outbursts. He snuck out of Hell and began a war in the mortal realm. He raised an army and taught them to revel in destruction. He sowed seeds of discord that last today. Feeling triumphant and invincible, Angels met him on the battlefield. They tore his demonic soul from his body and trapped it within a mountain, turning it into a volcano.

"The third son stands before me, born from a woman Satan tempted in a garden. He took the form of a talking serpent. He was the color of the sun with a black underbelly. The serpent spoke words of seduction and hypnotized the woman. When she fell asleep beneath an apple tree, he flicked his tongue at her sweet maidenhood, causing her to moan in delight. He wiggled his tail into her core until he breached her womb. He laid his eggs within her and remained inside her until she awakened. When he pulled out, he bit her breast, injecting her with his poison. The antidote was inside the ruby-red apples hanging from the very tree she slept beneath. She had the option to eat the apple and be cured and bear Satan's heirs or die. Naturally, she chose life.

"The fourth son of Satan was born to be his mother's favorite, as his older brother tore her body apart as he left the womb. His older brother was driven mad by jealousy of his younger brother. Watching him be praised while yearning for even a kind word from his mother awakened the beast within him. One day, he picked up a bone shard and lured his brother into a wheat field. His fury was unleashed as he continually stabbed his brother, laughing while his brother screamed.

"The youngest son of Satan was sired not through deception, but a relationship between Satan and a purebred angel. They met in the mortal realm and spent several days together. She gave her innocence to him and became pregnant with his heir. He returned to Hell until the angel gave birth. Eventually, he returned to see his son and became disgusted as the boy tried to hug his father. When his mother was called to ascend and accept her wings, she abandoned her boy in Hell.

"The angels weep for the children of Satan, as they are not to blame for that which they have done. Would you beat a lamb for unwittingly walking into the jaws of a wolf? Yet Satan has forsaken each of his children."

The oracle unwrapped the baby and stroked a bony finger across its forehead and watched tiny horns bud from its forehead. It's tail grew and wrapped around her wrist as she slapped it on the ass. The oracle nodded in approval.

"You children are blinded by your hatred. You feel you are entitled to something, though you haven't earned it. This child has already fought for life and will continue to do so."

Her wizened hand stroked the baby's back before withdrawing a hidden dagger from the folds of her flowing gown, which resembled the intricate webbing of spiders. Inhuman screams came from the child as she used the dagger to etch into the baby's spine.

"Hush now, little one. Your wings were bound."

A pair of tiny ethereal appendages sprouted from the baby's back where the oracle's deft cuts had been made. The wings were delicate and adorned with feathers of the softest pastel hues. The wings seemed to shimmer and catch the light.

"*She* will usher in a new era for all worlds."

The significance of the oracle's words echoed around them.

Lucifer

DESPERATION once again guided Lucien as he made his way to see the oracle. It had been hundreds of years since he'd last sought her counsel. But now, he needed to find a way to free Sadie once and for all.

When his mother offered him the crystal to bring Sadie back to say goodbye, he didn't give a damn about the consequences. He died every time she did. He mourned the loss of her smile and sincere nature as lies continued to fall off his tongue.

"I've been waiting for you," an eerie voice whispered.

"Revered Mother," he said as he dropped to his knee before the elderly woman sitting upon a gnarled stump.

"The son of Satan is humble enough to bow from his throne. I was right to mentor you."

The fog around them dissipated, revealing the dense forest around them. Knotty pines stood like gnarled sentinels, obscuring natural light, holding its secrets close. Only the oracle could give Lucifer the answers he sought.

"Tell me what I need to do. I will sacrifice anything."

"Are you willing to forgive yourself? You chose your own fate when your lover was dying in your arms. She would've earned wings if she had ascended like your mother, and you were fearful of allowing this. You intervened with divine fate and damned you both."

Tears flowed freely from Lucifer's eyes. She was saying everything he already knew, and it tore him up inside. The guilt that churned within his gut had driven him to commit unspeakable acts to which there was no contrition. The devil had fallen in love with an angel, but they were never meant to be together.

"I would've never seen her again," he confessed.

"Tell me, Lucifer. Can an innocent soul escape Hell unscathed?"

"She has to. I'll spend all of eternity making it up to her."

"And what if she doesn't want to rule Hell at your side? Do you love her enough to let her go?" She raised her all-seeing eyes to his.

"You already know the answer to that."

"Good. Your devotion speaks volumes of who you are. The son of a devil and an angel doesn't have to choose one side or the other. The war will tear you apart if you let it."

"Where is my son?"

She chuckled. "You continue to make assumptions. I have ensured your child's safety. When the time is right, I will reunite you. Until then, you have work to do."

"Sadie has one circle of Hell left. I will ensure she emerges triumphant."

"Tread carefully, son of Satan. Beware the face of deception as your biggest trial lies ahead."

ONCE HE STEPPED out of the oracle's glen, the fog obscured the land once more, hiding her from sight. She was protected by the elements that surrounded her and wouldn't be found again until she wanted to be. She saw a single thread of fate that could be unwound in thousands of different directions stemming from one single choice.

Her answers were cryptic, offering counsel and ominous warnings. She never intervened directly. It was for him to decipher the wisdom she imparted upon him. It was a small comfort knowing his child was under her care. But that also meant she knew he had more to do—Sadie had more to do.

He closed his eyes and laid his hand over his chest as his heart began thumping once more. He remained still for a few beats, reveling in the feelings only Sadie awakened before a smile spread across his face. If Lucifer had any say in the matter, this would be their final goodbye.

For hundreds of years, Sadie wept, telling him she didn't want to leave. It was his own inadequacies and guilt that propelled his actions. He told himself he did the right thing by her, but that was a lie. He meant what he said, that he would spend the rest of eternity making it up to her.

Lucifer was the one who needed healing, and Sadie was the only one who could grant him absolution. When they were reunited, they would hunt down Cain and Constance together. Retribution would be theirs. He would lay waste to the mortal realm and watch his beloved rise from the ashes.

He opened his eyes and couldn't believe the fortuitous sight before him. Constance appeared in the forest, looking lost and alone. He blinked multiple times to dispel the disbelief. She wasn't an illusion.

A growl rumbled deep within his chest. It was the first time he'd seen her since he threw her out of the castle with Sadie's weight in gold, and 500 years without his beloved had him thirsty for blood.

Her golden hair was a beacon through the fog, and the fine blue cloak she wore concealed her body as she turned in his direction. Recognition flashed across her face a moment before she ran toward him.

His heart beat furiously at her audacity. How dare she approach him. But it didn't matter. He licked his lips like a hungry predator. He was going to make her suffer and present Sadie with a lock of her hair.

Lucifer used the fog and the forest to his advantage and hid quickly. She tutted not far from where he had first stood. He remained close to the trees as he circled her, watching as she wandered aimlessly once more. She didn't call out, but she wasn't silent, either.

His ears strained to listen for every breath and heartbeat as hatred pumped through his veins. Anticipation bubbled beneath his skin, causing his horns to sprout. The demon within him was happy to see her. *Blood, blood,* it called, longing to be sated.

Constance froze as though sensing him behind her. She turned a moment too late and didn't have time to scream as his hands wrapped around her throat. Her eyes went wide with fear, knowing her life was about to end.

"Luci—" she croaked.

"Shut the fuck up, cunt," he growled. "I'm going to fucking kill you."

His pain manifested in a mighty roar, and his form shifted completely. He'd made a vow once and was determined to make her suffer. He laughed as she clawed at his giant hands. It was like a tickle from a kitten.

He lifted her a foot off the ground and threw her into a tree hard enough that the bark cracked. She fell to the forest floor with a cry. The ground quaked with every step Lucifer took as he approached, towering over the cowering woman.

"Please," she cried, raising her hands to shield herself, much like her mother had.

The more she begged, the more sick pleasure he would gain from their encounter. He wanted to pull her beating heart from her chest and savor its final beats before devouring it. He could feel the weight and warmth in his palm already and imagined the blood dripping from his fingertips.

Constance shrieked as he grabbed her hair and yanked so hard that a fistful came with it. With a swipe of his claws, he shredded her blue cloak and tore her gown, leaving her naked and trembling before him. He had expected more as his eyes trailed over her pale skin. Her breasts were small with tiny pink nipples, and the ringlets between her legs weren't enticing. She didn't compare to the beauty of her sister.

"You're at my mercy now," he hissed. "And there isn't a shred of it left."

"Look at me," she pleaded.

He ignored her and grinned sickly as he caressed her skin with his long dark nails. Once the demon awakened, it demanded blood and sacrifice. He was only too happy to rip Constance's soul from her body and damn it to Hell.

"Scream for me," he growled.

He dug his claw into her breast and sliced down her belly, just like she had done to her sister. How symbolic that she faced the same fate. Her shrieks and sobs were a perfect melody of pain and agony.

"Stop!" She screamed.

She fought hard, but he wasn't to be deterred. Constance grew weaker as the blood pooled around her, seeping into the ground. He watched the viscous liquid drip down his arms.

"Look at me, please," she begged through tears.

She could plead all she wanted, but he wouldn't stop. He was possessed with vengeance. Her ear-piercing screams echoed around them as he dug deeper.

"Lucien," she sobbed.

Only one person had ever cried his name with such desperation before. The demon paused as a cold shiver rolled down his burning back. Reality culled his bloodlust as his heart slowed painfully in his chest.

Lucifer looked into the eyes of the broken body in his arms as a painful tale was retold once more. How many times had those hazel eyes shone up at him with trust, vulnerability, love, and pain? How did he mistake them for blue? And the hair around her shoulders in disarray wasn't blonde but black.

He shook his head. It couldn't be. A faint smile ghosted her lips, daring to assuage his guilt as she died. He deserved to be flayed and punished for eternity.

"I'm sorry, Sadie. I'm sorry."

"I love you, Luci—"

And she was gone again. He howled like a beast as blinding pain ran through him. Lucifer's heart stopped beating.

"Sadie," he bellowed.

What had he done?

"Beware the face of deception," the oracle had warned him.

Lucifer had damned them both, and this would be the last time he lost her.

He stole all of Sadie's memories and held them within his soul. Whether or not she remembered him, they were bound for eternity. He wouldn't misplace his faith in her again.

"Wait for me, tulip."

He held her long after her body went cold once more. Sadie's soul had already slipped into the next trial—lust.

Twisted Games of Fate

Can an Innocent soul escape hell unscathed?

Love is a fallacy, as Lucien, the son of Satan, had come to learn. He fell in love with an angel and promised her eternity. Instead, he condemned her to hell for 500 years.

Sadie Winters gave her heart, body, and soul to the devil and was punished for it. She was thrust into the trials of The Society only to face a perpetual cycle of torture and death.

With The Society pressuring Sadie with false promises, she faces an impossible choice: accept their invitation or forget who she is once more.

Now, they must fight for love and reconciliation while facing their biggest trial yet.

Author's Note

The reading order for *The Twisted Society* series is as follows:

The Winter Maiden

The Initiate Rises

Scream at the Fair

Twisted Games of Fate

Society in Ruin

Originally, *Scream at the Fair* was meant to be a short, erotic holiday romance. As I wrote it, Lucien kept telling me he wouldn't be ignored. By the end, this couple begged for me to tell their beautifully twisted love story.

Buckle up, because this wild ride isn't over yet.

About the Author

Cristina Lollabrigida specializes in books that are romantic and smutty and will leave you with feels. She is best known for twists that will leave readers thirsting for more.

Originally from Chicago, Cristina is a country girl at heart. She currently lives with her husband and their three children in South Carolina. And when she's not writing, she's reading romance novels.

Also by Cristina Lollabrigida

The Twisted Society

Scream at the Fair

WHAT WOULD YOU DO FOR $100,000?

Tallulah Daniels has been contacted by the mysterious Society. A $100,000 prize is hers if she can survive 12 hours in the abandoned fairgrounds. It should be easy for a horror movie buff to spend her Halloween being scared by actors.

It turns out to be more than jump scares and costume makeup. She's trapped in a sensual nightmare and pushed to her limits. When quitting isn't an option, will the seductive Lucien turn out to be friend or foe as Tallulah attempts to elude her masked hunters?

The Winter Maiden

The Winter Maiden has been chosen...

Sadie Winters was born into submission, made to remain in the shadows, unseen and unheard. Her compassionate nature led to a chance encounter with one of her masters and changed her life forever.

Cain, the eldest son of a Society member, locks Sadie away and claims her as his. She wishes for death until she meets his brother, Lucien.

A forbidden love affair erupts between captive and master, leaving Sadie caught between brothers. When she discovers the truth about The Society, it becomes a race for survival in a game where there are no winners.

Twisted Games of Fate (Summer 2024)

Can an Innocent soul escape hell unscathed?

Love is a fallacy, as Lucien, the son of Satan, had come to learn. He fell in love with an angel and promised her eternity. Instead, he condemned her to hell for 500 years.

Sadie Winters gave her heart, body, and soul to the devil and was punished for it. She was thrust into the trials of The Society only to face a perpetual cycle of torture and death.

With The Society pressuring Sadie with false promises, she faces an impossible choice: accept their invitation or forget who she is once more.

Now, they must fight for love and reconciliation while facing their biggest trial yet.

Society in Ruin

Fall 2024

Dark Romances

Accidental Bride

Upholding the law was all Drake Walker ever wanted to do. Until he found himself married to the one person that could ruin him...

Marriage by Trial

Tired of being used as a pawn in everyone's plan, Alessandra decides it's time to take her future in her own hands, even if it means burning down the world around her.

You're My Always

To have, to hold, and to protect... Always.

Contemporary Romances

Running After You

Cinnamon Roll Hero (sin-a-mon roll he-ro): (n) a hero who is too sweet for this world...but will fight to the death for the people they care about.

Princess for a Day

True love, royal intrigue, and the adventure of a lifetime await!

Lake Heart

Sometimes your true dream is the one you leave behind.

Made in the USA
Columbia, SC
12 August 2024

39905955R00050